PERRY PANDA

A Story about Parental Depression

Helen Bashford

Illustrated by Russell Scott-Skinner

Jessica Kingsley Publishers
London and Philadelphia

This edition first published in 2018
by Jessica Kingsley Publishers
73 Collier Street
London N1 9BE, UK
and
400 Market Street, Suite 400
Philadelphia, PA 19106, USA

www.jkp.com

Library of Congress Cataloging in Publication Data
A CIP catalog record for this book is available from the Library of Congress

British Library Cataloguing in Publication Data
A CIP catalogue record for this book is available from the British Library

ISBN 978 1 78592 412 5
eISBN 978 1 78450 773 2

Printed and bound in China

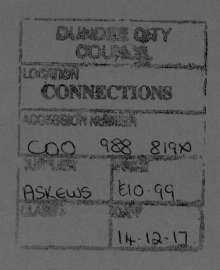

For Finlay, Cleo and Arthur

Perry Panda's mummy
treats him like a star.
She chats
and laughs
and reads with him.
She's the best mummy by far!

He doesn't understand it
and feels really quite confused.
He wonders what has happened
to make mummy feel so bruised.

So Perry has a long hard think
about what makes her so sad.
And then he starts to wonder,
"Is it because I'm bad?"

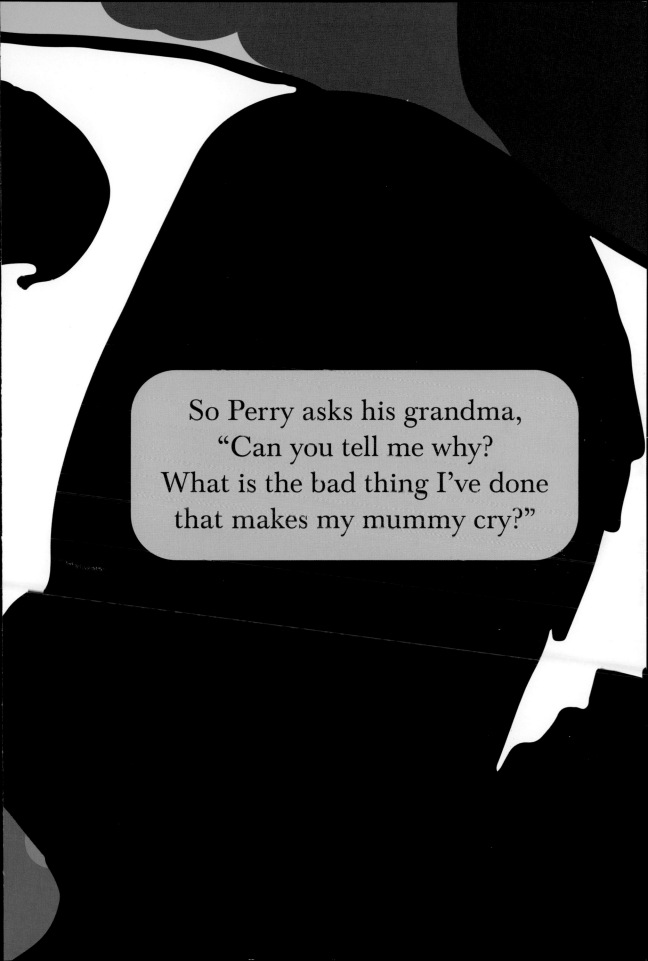

Perry Panda's grandma
pulls him up upon her knee.
She gives him a great big panda hug,
"Now listen here to me...

It's not because of children
if mummies are very sad.
It's not because of children
if mummies seem very mad.

Perry, you're not naughty
and you've not upset your mum.
It's not your fault
– it's never your fault –
that your mummy feels this glum.

Sometimes mums get very sad
because other things went wrong.
Perhaps they got some bad, bad news,
or heard a tearful song.

"So how can we help my mum?"
asked Perry of his gran.
"There must be something we can do.
We'll help – I know we can!"

"Making a panda feel better
might mean taking daily pills.
It might mean talking or lots of sleep,
or walking in the hills.

It could be that a hospital stay
will help them feel just right.
But often it takes a long, long time
and feels like quite a fight.

So Perry has a long hard think
about what he could do to help.
He thinks and thinks,
and thinks some more,
then lets out an excited yelp.

There's nothing that feels better
than cuddles, warm and snug.
So he runs upstairs to find his mum
and gives her a great big hug.

For more information on the issues covered in
Perry Panda and links to organisations for support,
visit www.perrypanda.com.

About the Author and Illustrator

Helen Bashford has experience working in the
mental health field, most recently as Carers Lead
for a Mental Health Trust, providing support for
families. She lives in Kent, UK.

Russell Scott-Skinner is an artist based in Kent, UK.